FAQ

TEEN LIFE™

FREQUENTLY ASKED QUESTIONS ABOUT

Cyberbullying

Teri Breguet

ROSEN
PUBLISHING®

New York

For anyone who has ever been bullied

Published in 2007 by The Rosen Publishing Group, Inc.
29 East 21st Street, New York, NY 10010

Library of Congress Cataloging-in-Publication Data

Breguet, Teri.
Frequently asked questions about cyberbullying / by Teri Breguet.—1st ed.
p. cm.—(FAQ: teen life)
Includes bibliographical references and index.
ISBN-13: 978-1-4042-0963-3
ISBN-10: 1-4042-0963-8 (lib. bdg.)
1. Cyberbullying. 2. Computer crimes. 3. Technology and law. I. Title.
HV6773.B74 2007
302.3—dc22

2006020875

Manufactured in the United States of America

Contents

Introduction

You might have seen the humiliation, experienced it yourself as a victim, or maybe even participated in picking on another person. Most people have witnessed bullying. A friend may have been teased for being different, be it that he didn't dress like the others or had few friends. A group of boys might have called a girl names in front of other people to embarrass her. Most of us have seen somebody get taunted, and unfortunately, we will probably see it time and time again throughout our entire lives.

Bullying is a method of intimidation that takes many forms and has existed through the generations. Traditionally, bullying takes place outside the home, among a victim's peer group, and in a public place such as school. For the victims of bullying, they could get away from the harassment by running to the safety of their homes.

A new form of bullying has begun to take shape that may be even harsher than the traditional kind. The victim is unable to escape the harassment easily, and the humiliation doesn't necessarily end after the crowd of onlookers disperses. In cyberbullying, bullies use computers to send threatening e-mails and cell phones to take digital pictures of their victims that they manipulate and later post online. They also torment their victims by constantly showing up in chat rooms where they can be found.

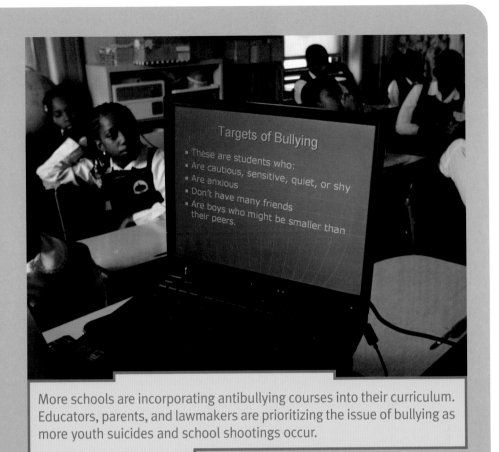

More schools are incorporating antibullying courses into their curriculum. Educators, parents, and lawmakers are prioritizing the issue of bullying as more youth suicides and school shootings occur.

Cyberbullying is a form of bullying in which the perpetrator chooses to harass his or her victim through a technological device. For the bully, there are several reasons he or she may choose this form of bullying. It can be done anonymously, it can be done with little effort, and the harassment can be carried out repeatedly and at a convenient time for the bully. Perhaps most appealing to the bully, there is a constant, captive audience to witness his or her handiwork and the victim's humiliation.

The victim's way out may seem simple: ignore the behavior by turning off the computer or cell phone. However, research and experiences are proving that this approach is not effective enough to get rid of the dogged bully. If you find yourself in a situation in which somebody is harassing you, get help. Cyberbullying is difficult to escape, is emotionally hurtful, and is illegal. Know your rights, understand your options, and end the cycle of harassment.

WHAT IS CYBERBULLYING?

Most people can't remember what daily life was like before the cell phone and the Internet became widely available. Because of this communication technology, a person can easily find information on almost anything, comparison shop for airline tickets, stay in touch with people far away without having to pick up pen and paper, and be able to reach a person throughout the day.

With these advantages come an unfortunate number of ways in which the new capacity for speed, reach, and convenience is abused. Sexual predators use the Internet to reach out to potential victims. Hackers develop viruses to destroy important information. People tap into Web sites to steal a person's identity. Cyberbullying is one more way that technology is misused. For the bullies who want to see somebody get hurt, there are many means in which they can bombard a victim with cruel messages and disturbing images, and broadcast the victim's embarrassing moments for others to see. In the hands of the cyberbully, the Internet, the cell phone, and other technologies are not just convenient tools, they're also handy vehicles to get to his or her victims.

According to *District Administration* magazine, not only is cyberbullying invasive, it's also very common: most twelve- to fourteen-year-olds say they have been cyberbullied. Experts say that while cyberbullying can begin at any age, it is more commonly reported by children who are around nine years old. Studies suggest that it is around this age that children begin having more freedom on the Internet. Also, as they embark on adolescence, they gain more independence from adult supervision.

Online Cyberbullying

The Internet provides many outlets for cyberbullies' aggression. Although there are many ways in which a person could use the Internet to hurt someone, there are two main types of online harassment: cyberthreats and cyberstalking.

Cyberthreats include information posted online that agitates a person or a group of people to inflict violence against a targeted victim. They may also include messages that pressure the victim to inflict self-harm. There are two kinds of cyberthreats. The first kind is a direct threat. When somebody makes a direct threat, he or she bluntly states his or her intentions of wanting to hurt somebody else or him or herself. Examples of direct threats are, "I am going to kill you" or "I am going to end my life."

Pay attention to your reaction to an e-mail. If it makes you uncomfortable, this could be a sign that the message is threatening in nature.

The other kind of cyberthreat, an indirect threat, takes a bit of reading between the lines. For example, someone who may be considering suicide might say, "What is the point of living? The world would be better off without me." This type of threat is just as much a cry for help. Another example of an indirect threat could be, "I hate you. I wish you would just go away." The person making the threat  may not be directly warning a person, but the idea of harm is still present.

Traditional stalking takes the form of harassment that threatens harm or is highly intimidating, often including intrusion of someone's privacy. Harassment is defined as the act of annoying someone continually by pestering or teasing him or her. When someone stalks another person, he or she generally follows the victim, appearing at the victim's home or workplace, or by making repeated telephone calls to the victim. A cyberstalker does the same thing electronically. He or she stalks a person using the Internet or other electronic devices. For example, a victim of cyberstalking may receive an e-mail with a particular threat, then turn on his or her cell phone and see the message again and again. A victim feels intimidated because he or she feels followed and unable to escape.

In other cases, a guy may be in love with a particular girl, and she does not feel the same way, or vice versa. The guy feels hurt and wants to get back at the girl for not returning his feelings. He may turn to stalking because it gives him a sense of control over her life. He does not want her to be happy or have privacy. A cyberstalker might say, "I am watching you. I know what you are doing."

Chat Room Bullying

Most victims of cyberbullying say abuse occurs in chat rooms, where people who are in the virtual rooms send and receive messages, called "chatting." Some chat rooms center around a topic, like a particular rock band, or they can be rooms that don't have a conversational theme. Popular chat rooms can be filled with hundreds of people at one time. People "inside" chat rooms generally use screen names, or nicknames, and all the screen names of people in the chat room are listed on each user's screen. A person can read messages from others in the chat room and type and send his or her message as a reply. What someone types appears instantly on the screen as part of the chat.

When cyberbullies send rude or obscene messages directed at a person, it is called "flaming." For example, a fifth grader

> It is easy to get lured into participating in cyberbullying without even realizing it. If somebody is making fun of another person, the best thing to do is to refrain from reacting.

who received an instant message that warned, "Watch your back in the hallways," according to *Current Health 2* magazine, was threatened through flaming.

A common method of cyberbullying in the chat room is for the bully to engage someone in a conversation and trick him or her into revealing private information. The bully might save the conversation and forward what was thought to be revealed in confidence for others to read, exposing the victim's secrets.

Sharing someone's embarrassing secrets or images is called "outing." A cyberbully who "outs" his or her victim may pose as a friend long enough to gain the victim's trust. For example, a cruel girl might trick a boy who she knows has a crush on her by engaging him in a chat. He soon believes she likes him. He tells her about his personal life, maybe about his parents' divorce and that he's on antidepression medication. She then

Myths and Facts
About Cyberbullying

Cyberbullies are usually people who are popular, athletic, and attractive. Fact ➡ Cyberbullies come in all shapes and sizes. Because people who cyberbully can hide behind their anonymity, they are often physically weak and socially awkward. Often, they are the victims of traditional bullying who turn to cyberbullying to get revenge.

Young people are rarely the cyberbullies. Fact ➡ Although they may not always be the main perpetrators, 53 percent of students in fourth to eighth grade admit that they have said mean or hurtful things to someone online. Another 5 percent admit that they participate in cyberbullying "quite often," according to the publication *Reclaiming Children and Youth*.

Most teens will not experience cyberbullying. Fact ➡ Recent surveys conducted by Internet safety organizations show that more than 50

percent of adolescents experience some form of cyberbullying. Many times, it begins as early as age nine. In the teen years, cyberbullying usually accompanies some form of sexual harassment.

 More boys than girls participate in cyberbullying.
Fact ➠ Boys and girls participate in cyberbullying equally, although for different reasons. They also use different methods. Girls tend to use more passive approaches, like spreading rumors and gossip to damage reputations and relationships. Boys tend to use direct threats and cyberbully as a means of revenge.

 Children rarely miss school to avoid bullying.
Fact ➠ Educators estimate that more than 160,000 students miss school each day in the United States because they fear being bullied or harassed by their peers, according to the publication *InternetWeek*.

· ·

posts his secrets for everyone to see, calling him "crazy." She might even trick him into sending her a photo of himself, and then she posts it online to make fun of him.

In some cases, the victim isn't somebody the cyberbully knows. A person can easily get lured into participation without even knowing it. Known as "trolling," cyberbullies deliberately post false information in the hopes of getting innocent people to respond and contribute to a discussion that serves to harass a victim.

E-mail Cyberbullying

More than half of cyberbullying victims say the abuse happens online. About 28 percent of youth said they were bullied through e-mail in a 2005 survey from the Web site www.cyberbullying.us. Cyberbullies might break into e-mail accounts. One tactic of hackers (those who steal private information online) is to send an anonymous e-mail to unsuspecting people. When the receiver opens the e-mail, it enables the hacker to get information about that e-mail account. A cyberbully might also impersonate his or her victim after breaking into an e-mail account. The bully might pose as the e-mail account owner and send messages to make the person look bad or get the victim into trouble.

Web Site Cyberbullying

A "bash board" is a type of online bulletin board in which people can post their thoughts and opinions. Bash board postings are generally malicious and hateful statements directed against another person.

A cyberbully might create Web sites that contain stories and jokes or depict cartoons and pictures ridiculing his or her victims. Some Web log writers dedicate whole pages to "anyone and everyone they hate and why," according to *Current Health 2* magazine. Posting pictures of classmates online and asking people to rate them or posting demeaning questions are other examples of cyberbullying.

Exclusion

A person can be bullied without even having interaction with a bully. A person who is purposely left out is also a victim of cyberbullying. Known as "exclusion," some bullies deliberately exclude someone from an instant messaging (IM) group, like a "buddy list," to hurt his or her feelings.

Social networking Web sites such as Facebook and MySpace are places where a person might be excluded. Users on these interactive Web sites build a community in which its members know what is going on in a person's life through pictures, Web logs, and bulletin messages that users post. It is very hurtful to the person who is denied acceptance into these online communities.

Cell Phone Cyberbullying

You and your "wired" friends are probably able to be reached, or able to communicate to others, throughout most of the day. It is for this reason that cyberbullying is a frustrating problem. The fact that a cell phone is never far from its owner makes that person a perpetual target of victimization. It also makes the cell phone an easy tool for abuse. People with cell phones usually keep them turned on, which provides cyberbullies the opportunity to threaten and insult them whenever they want. This also means that the victim can't escape the harassment, even at

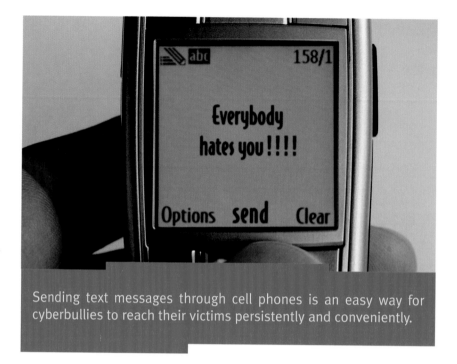

Sending text messages through cell phones is an easy way for cyberbullies to reach their victims persistently and conveniently.

home. If the cyberbully is determined enough, he or she can intimidate the victim all the time.

Text Messages

Text messages are electronic messages that are sent either online or from a cell phone to another cell phone. About 49 percent of cyberbullying victims say they are bullied through text messages sent through computers, according to cyberbullying.us. This high number is probably due to two reasons: text messaging guarantees that the victim will receive the threat, and it is easy for the bully to do. Most people shut off their computers when they are done using them, but people leave their cell phones on at all times.

Cyberbullies take advantage of this. For example, a cyberbully may know when his or her victim is at work or may be at an important social function. The person will send a cruel message to ruin the victim's good time.

Digital Photos

Cyberbullying is cruel, but it is especially hurtful for self-conscious teenage victims when it involves digital photos. Cyberbullies might capture their victims as they are changing in the school locker room or are using the bathroom. If the cyberbully used a cell phone to take the picture, he or she can share the photo immediately with others by sending it to other cell phones, e-mail accounts, or posting it online.

Bullies also scan pictures of his or her victims and manipulate the photographs. These cyberbullies might alter their victim's appearance or change their victim's actions in the photo, making it seem like the person was engaging in embarrassing or illegal behavior.

Cyberbullies might also engage in "happy slapping." This is an extreme form of bullying in which the bully physically assaults his or her victim and records the beating with a cell phone. Later, the bully distributes the recording so that others can watch the assault.

chapter two

WHO ARE CYBERBULLIES AND THEIR VICTIMS?

The attraction that prods the traditional bully is the same for a cyberbully. The bully takes advantage of his or her victim's weakness to intimidate and gain power over the victim. Whereas traditional bullying consists of malicious intent and verbal or physical abuse, repeated over time, cyberbullying is willful and repeated harm inflicted through a technological device. Cyberbullies, while similar to traditional bullies in their intent to hurt others through power and control, are different in that they use technology as the vehicle to harass.

Cyberbullying victims feel especially trapped and invaded. In fact, recent studies have shown that most teenagers believe that online bullying is as bad, if not worse, than "real-life" bullying because it invades the home. There is no escape from it when technology is everywhere.

> Cyberbullies are usually people who are picked on by playground bullies. Unlike the traditional bully, who is usually stronger, cyberbullies don't use size to intimidate their victims.

Why Do People Cyberbully?

Unlike the playground bully, who is usually bigger and stronger than his or her class-mates, the cyberbully can be anyone. Cyberbullying is especially attractive because technology allows anonymity. Temporary e-mail accounts and chat room pseudonyms can help keep a person's identity hidden. This ability to hide makes cyberbullies all the bolder. It takes less energy and courage to express hurtful comments using a keyboard than with a voice.

Many refer to cyberbullying as a type of revenge used by the underdogs. Through cyberbullying, people who have been picked on can retaliate by picking on their attackers, or by picking on somebody they perceive as weaker than they are. Because technology acts as a buffer between the bully and the victim, cyberbullies might even feel that what they are doing is not harmful. They don't see their victim's tears or the other signs of distress that they've caused with their tormenting.

Who Are Cyberbullies?

It is difficult to get a clear-cut profile of cyberbullies because they remain anonymous unless they are caught. For that reason, there is conflicting information about the typical cyberbully. Cyberbullies are usually preteens and teens who are smart and technologically savvy. They are typically the "nerds" because with cyberbullying, they have a chance of anonymous retaliation against those who have picked on them. Cyberbullies can be, however, predators of any age looking for someone vulnerable.

Most cyberbullies know their victims in some capacity. They could "meet" their victim in an online chat room, or their victims could be ex-boyfriends or ex-girlfriends. Serial bullies are serial attention seekers. It doesn't matter what type of attention they get, positive or negative, as long as they can provoke someone and have the power to control another person's moves.

Bullies, especially cyberbullies, are known to be obsessive people. For example, a cyberbully who has been caught and has his or her e-mail account closed down might just open a new account and employ the same words, phrases, and strategies, not even attempting to hide behind new tactics.

It's important to keep in mind that people are not born bullies. Bullying is usually a result of a cycle of learned behavior. Sadly, bullies often experience bullying at home by their own parents or a sibling. They then apply their learned behavior onto others.

Bullying of any kind stems from learned behavior that generally begins during a young age. There are instances of people who were bullied their entire lives and eventually committed suicide.

Parents of bullies often support their children's aggressive behavior. For this reason, bullies have no sense of remorse for hurting someone, and they often refuse to accept responsibility for their wrong behavior. In fact, because people they trust accept the way that they act, they may not even fully accept that bullying another person is wrong and cruel. With the right approach, however, bullying behavior can be changed.

People who bully at an early age tend to become aggressive adults if they don't do anything about their behavior. Bullies usually continue to find victims throughout their lives. They bully their classmates, spouses, children, and sometimes their coworkers.

SHERRY'S STORY

"It was awful. It was simply awful."

That is what Sherry remembers of her time in grade school several years ago. The popular girls would follow her around at recess and in the hallways at school, taunting her because she was so quiet and because they thought her clothes were ugly. Sherry's family did not have much money, so she didn't wear the same type of clothes her peers wore.

What Sherry did like was to learn new things, and she liked school. She often raised her hand in class when her teachers asked questions. Her classmates began calling her "Miss Know It All." Sherry did not mean to "show off" her intelligence. She just liked learning. Despite the problems she had at school, she was content going home to study and spend time with her family.

Then puberty struck during the fifth grade. When she was eleven, Sherry began developing earlier than her classmates. At first, they teased her about parts of her body and then about her sexuality. The bullying became cruel.

"The boys threw pennies at me in the hallways," she recalls. "I didn't leave my room for a couple months after it happened."

Sherry felt physically sick to her stomach whenever she thought of returning to school. She told her parents, and they spoke with her teachers and the principal. The bullying seemed to happen less.

Several years later, Sherry began high school. She was no longer the "nerdy" girl the others teased. Sherry had many friends, and she had blossomed into a tall young woman. Sherry was excited about high school. She wanted to be a doctor, and college was not far off now. Her parents rewarded her good grades by buying her a computer. Each night, she would go into chat rooms to send instant messages with her friends before bed.

One night, Sherry stumbled onto a home page where boys from her school had posted pictures of her. They wrote all kinds of things about her body. They thought she was "hot."

"Some of my friends said I should be excited that guys think of me that way. But it wasn't like that," she says. "It was hurtful."

Sherry became angry at her classmates who were hiding behind their computer screens. She did not trust anyone anymore.

The traditional bullying may have stopped in middle school, but now her classmates were using the Internet to harass her. Again, Sherry started staying home from school. She was self-conscious and afraid of all the boys now. What if one of them actually tried to do one of the things he fantasized about on the Web site?

Sherry wanted to tell her parents again. This time, she was afraid they would think she caused the problem somehow. Maybe they would take her computer away. Maybe they would punish her. But she knew she had a good relationship with them and she was confident she did nothing wrong, so she told them.

Sherry's parents helped her trace the identity of the boys who made the Web site. They then informed the school and sent a letter to the boys' parents. The letter included printouts of the Web site and a request that the cyberbullying stop immediately. Shortly there-after, it did. Just to be safe, though, Sherry still avoids certain chat rooms and home pages.

Female Bullies

Studies show that cyberbullying is done by both girls and boys, although in different ways and for different reasons. Girl cyberbullies tend to use more passive approaches. They are more likely to spread rumors and malicious gossip, and use sexual innuendo. The female cyberbully prefers relational bullying, meaning her goal is to destroy her victim's social life. According to the Web site www.stopcyberbullying.org, girls tend to cyberbully through offensive messages sent to their victims or posted publicly.

The American Educational Research Association found that self-identified female bullies most often use their cell phones to send cruel text messages to their peers, saying they prefer this over using the Internet. About 45 percent of those female bullies surveyed admitted to being victims of cyberbullying themselves.

One seventeen-year-old girl explained on cyberbullying.us why she felt tempted to cyberbully. "I had recently picked on an old friend of mine, for what I will not reveal . . . I was disappointed she was not my friend any longer so I spread her deepest secrets to everyone, which made her feel guilty because I had known her for years. At the same time, it was payback time so people know not to attempt to mess around with me."

"Cyberbullying in the hands of girls can be particularly devastating. After all, it is coming at a time when peer group acceptance is highly sought. Girls share so much information when they are friends that they never run out of ammunition if they turn on one another," says Richard Sarles, a professor of psychiatry and pediatrics at the University of Maryland in Baltimore, in "Wired Kids, Inc."

Male Bullies

Boys who bully, both the traditional and cyber kind, tend to be more direct and aggressive than girls. Boys are more apt to intimidate their victims by engaging in name-calling and through malicious teasing and obscene and threatening gestures. Typically, male cyberbullies use the computer more than the cell phone. If they do use their cell phones, they usually use them to take digital pictures. Boys tend to send one-on-one messages, pass around offensive images, and steal passwords and hack into others' systems. A common tactic that boys use is exclusion. Here's an example that was posted on cyberbully.org.

Michael beat another boy in an online game. Several of the friends of the boy who lost started threatening Michael in the game's chat room. "We'll make you pay for this," they said. Now when Michael tries to play on that site, a group of other players gang up on him and restrict his activities so he cannot play.

Passive Participants

Bullies always like a crowd. Cyberbullies get a perverse sense of satisfaction from what they do, and they want others to see it. Onlookers are very important to the success of cyberbullying for this reason. Observers, whether they number 3 or 300, provide approval for the behavior to continue. Somebody who witnesses the taunting may know that the behavior is wrong, but if he or

Gossiping might seem like harmless fun, but it forms the kind of group mentality that leads several people to gang up on one person. If your friends are trying to spread rumors, just walk away.

she doesn't do anything to help the victim, that onlooker is a third-party participant in the bullying. Bystanders represent the largest group of participants in cyberbullying.

The Victims

Bullies do not necessarily pick on people with physical handicaps; they prefer the social handicaps. Victims tend to be shy and socially awkward. People who are bullied usually are not assertive and have low self-esteem and not many friends. The most common time for bullying behavior is in middle school, when a person's surging hormones cause embarrassing physical changes.

With traditional bullying, doctors and parents can often see symptoms. Children or adolescents who are being bullied at school are anxious. They may fake being sick and have unexplained cuts and bruises. In the case of cyberbullying, the scars run emotionally deep. Cyberbullying victims feel lonely, humiliated, and insecure—even more so than they may already feel. Children who are repeatedly bullied have low self-esteem and do not trust people. They may fear for their safety because of the harassment that they bear. Although they are doing nothing wrong, victims worry about getting punished by parents, teachers, or even the police.

Being cyberbullied and having few opportunities to get away from it cause a wide range of stress-related illnesses. A fourteen-year-old girl from Illinois shares her experience: "I still cry when I think of what she said. After a while, you start believing all of the things people tell you that aren't true." A peer from New Jersey sums it up on cyberbullying.us: "Being bullied over the Internet is worse . . . They say 'sticks and stones may break my bones, but words will never hurt me.' That quote is a lie and I don't believe it. Sticks and stones may cause nasty cuts and scars, but those cuts and scars will heal. Insulting words hurt and sometimes take forever to heal."

How Cyberbullying Affects Its Victims

Victims may become preoccupied with plotting ways to avoid certain peers in cyberspace and in real life. Victims are constantly worried about these things, causing poor grades and other problems. A cyberbullying.us study of 3,000 students revealed that 38 percent of bullying victims said they felt vengeful, 37 percent were angry, and 24 percent felt helpless. Male victims tend to feel angry and vengeful, while female victims tend to direct their feelings inward through self-pity and depression.

Many students may try to deny the seriousness of name-calling, teasing, and other related activities, but studies have found that 8 percent of participants admitted that traditional bullying affected them to the point of attempting suicide, running away, refusing to attend school, or becoming chronically ill, according to cyberbullying.us.

Cyberbullying Tragedies

In 2005, classmates taunted and teased a boy about his short height through instant messaging. After more than a month of harassment, the thirteen-year-old committed suicide.

In another case, peers repeatedly challenged a boy to kill himself through e-mails and IM. They dared and doubled-dared him, and told him he'd be a hero if he committed suicide. The boy never had many friends and saw this as his chance to fit in. "The only way to earn their respect is to kill myself," he said. Peer acceptance was so important, probably something he had never had in his whole life, that he took his own life in order to get it. (WiredKids.com)

People all have things they dream about, but one teen was punished for acting out an innocent and goofy fantasy. One day, he was fooling around with a video camera and taped himself reenacting a fight scene from the movie *Star Wars*. He

Judith Scruggs was convicted in Connecticut in 2003 of creating an unhealthy home environment that led to the suicide of her bullied twelve-year-old son.

never intended for anyone to see the videotape. Some classmates found it, however, and, as a prank, they uploaded it to an Internet file-sharing network.

It wasn't long before doctored versions of the tape were seen by millions worldwide. Like any sensitive teenager, the teen was mortified by the attention. His emotional state left him debilitated, and he finished the school year in a psychiatric hospital.

FAQ

TEEN LIFE™

FREQUENTLY ASKED QUESTIONS ABOUT

Cyberbullying

Teri Breguet

ROSEN
PUBLISHING®

New York

Identifying Threats

Knowing when to ignore insults and when to get help are vital to protecting yourself. You don't always recognize threats when you see them. But you can get some hints by asking yourself the following about a message that sounds alarms.

- Does it contain lewd language?
- Does it insult you directly? ("You are stupid!")
- Does it threaten you vaguely? ("I'm going to get you!")
- Does it threaten you with bodily harm or death? ("I'm going to beat you up!")
- Does it make a serious general threat? ("There is a bomb in the school!" or "Don't take the school bus today!")

Another way to determine whether you are being cyber-bullied is by the frequency of the messages. The more repeated the communications are, the greater the threat. How often are you being told these hurtful things? Was it just once? Twice? Are the threats increasing? Do other people appear to be joining in? Remember that onlookers provide fuel for the cyberbully.

Look at the nature of the threats. Does the cyberbully seem to pop up throughout the day, in chat rooms where you are signed in? Is he or she sending you repeated e-mails? Sometimes, cyberbullies will sign you up for pornography sites and e-mailing lists. If you start receiving something out of the ordinary, do not open it. Tell your parents or an adult.

Has your password been stolen, or have any of your accounts been tampered with? If you are receiving messages from a friend that don't sound like his or her usual e-mails, then a cyberbully may have broken into your friend's account and be impersonating him or her.

Bystanders are an important component to the cyberbully's feelings of success. Because they want their work to be seen, cyberbullies often encourage others to share their "hit lists." A hit list is a compilation of names of students and sometimes faculty members whom a cyberbully wants to harm or kill. Does your name appear on any lists? Has anyone posted nasty comments on your Web log or guest book? Is your name registered on a bash board, or has it been associated with rude or provocative comments you never made? Cyberbullies might insult a person on their own Web site and sign the posting using a different name.

Has anyone posed as you by stealing your IM name or e-mail account and broken the rules of a Web site or service by using profanity or illegally downloading material? Have you been the brunt of any jokes?

Physical Symptoms

Your general mood and physical health are good indicators of whether or not you are being harassed. Many cyberbullying victims constantly feel on edge, a term called hypervigilance. They have panic attacks, which make them sweat, shake, and have heart palpitations.

Victims of cyberbullying are often nervous and distracted and feel trapped. This can lead to depression and suicidal thoughts.

If you feel nervous when you receive e-mails, IMs, or text messages, or find yourself angry, depressed, or frustrated after you use the computer, then there is a good chance that your online activity is causing the distress.

Chat Room Acronyms

The language of many chat rooms consists of abbreviations. Cyberbullies will often use acronyms that indicate that they are enjoying watching their prey squirm. For example, BEG means

10 FACTS ABOUT CYBERBULLYING

1 Forty-two percent of teens say they have been bullied online. Of those teens, 20 percent have received mean or threatening e-mails, and 58 percent have not told their parents or another adult about their online experiences.

2 One out of four kids is bullied. Every seven minutes, a child is bullied with only 4 percent adult intervention; 11 percent peer intervention; and 85 percent with no intervention.

3 One out of five kids admits to being a bully or having done some bullying.

4 Up to 60 percent of people who are identified as childhood bullies have at least one criminal conviction by the age of twenty-four.

5 One hundred thousand students carry a gun to school. Twenty-eight percent of young people who carry weapons have witnessed violence at home.

6 Sixty percent of teen girls admit to having cybersex.

7 Ninety-three percent of video games reward violent behavior. Twenty-five percent of boys from ages twelve to seventeen regularly visit gore- and hate-related Web sites.

8 About 20 percent of people younger than eighteen received a sexual solicitation over the Internet in 2004, according to the U.S. Department of Justice's Office of Juvenile Justice and Delinquency Prevention. One in four girls and one in six boys admitted to meeting Internet strangers in person.

9 Eighty-seven percent of teens from ages twelve to seventeen use the Internet, compared to 66 percent of all adults. Half of those teenagers go online daily.

10 One-third of all preteens and teens in the United States have a cell phone. Thirty-three percent use text messaging regularly.

"big evil grin," and FOMCL stands for "falling off my chair laughing." LLTA denotes "lots and lots of thunderous applause," and WEG means "wicked evil grin." Someone in the chat room may be upset when they respond CRBT, meaning "crying real big tears." You can find lists of chat abbreviations on helpful Web sites such as http://www.cyberbullying.us and http://www.acronymsonline.com if you ever question what certain acronyms mean.

Although you may not know exactly who is in a certain chat room, you should be able to get a sense of the tone of the discussion. Profanities can be a clear indicator that those chatting are not the most respectful people. A good indicator that something could be wrong is if somebody writes PAW, "parents are watching," or YBS for "you'll be sorry."

Preventing Cyberbullying

If you are not a victim of cyberbullying, try to keep it that way. Begin practicing the following things to stay safe and to avoid becoming a victim:

- Never give out personal information online, whether in instant message profiles, chat rooms, Web logs, or personal Web sites.
- Never tell anyone but your parents your passwords, not even your friends.
- If someone sends a mean or threatening message, do not respond. Save it or print it out, and show it to an adult.
- Never open e-mail from someone you don't know or from someone you know is a bully.
- Don't put anything online that you wouldn't want your classmates to see, even in an e-mail.
- Don't send messages when you are angry. Before clicking "send," ask yourself how you would feel if you received that message.

Spam is unsolicited electronic mail sent from someone the receiver does not know. It is often a wise idea not to open spam. Not only might it come with undesirable messages, it can also come with a virus that can destroy valuable information on your hard drive or even cause your whole computer system to crash.

Tell an adult if you suspect someone you know is cyberbullying someone else. Some telltale signs are if the person quickly

Always tell a responsible adult if you experience any bullying behavior or suspect it may be happening to someone else.

switches screens or closes programs when you walk by, if he or she is always on the computer, if he or she is upset when the computer isn't available for use, if he or she laughs excessively while using the computer, if he or she avoids discussions about his or her activities on the computer, or if he or she is using multiple online accounts or an account that is not his or her own.

Help those who are being bullied online by not joining in. Show the bullying messages to an adult. It might help to use a computer that is located in a busy area of your home. You might have your own computer in your room, but you should still share what things you are doing online with your parents.

WHAT SHOULD I DO IF I AM BEING CYBERBULLIED?

If you are being harassed, the most important thing to do is to get help. You might be afraid to tell your parents or guardians because you fear you will get the blame and that your computer or cell phone will be taken away. You should be honest, and don't act as if you have something to hide. Tell an adult.

Tell the Chat Host

If you are being cyberbullied, try to find out the identity of your harasser. If you are being cyberbullied by somebody in a chat room, there is usually a chat "host" who "chaperones" the site's activities to keep communications safe. However, it is up to you to report bullying behavior, and oftentimes it will be up to you to trace and preserve incriminating evidence. Though the host's job is to police the site and evict offensive people who break proper "netiquette," or Internet etiquette, personal messages are viewable only by the sender and the recipient. This means the chat host cannot read the exchange. The host serves to punish those who break the rules, not to find the offenders. Unfortunately, for e-mails and text messages, there is no one to monitor or censor offensive content.

While law enforcement officials have much greater capabilities when it comes to identifying anonymous cyberbullies, there are some things you can do to gather information.

Tracing Internet Bullies

Even if a bully changes an e-mail address, the computer he or she used is still identifiable and can be tracked down. All computers on the Internet have what is called an IP, or Internet Protocol, address. IP addresses typically look something like this: 217.37.61.148.

This information is in e-mail headers, which contain the technical information about the message, like the identity of the sender and the recipient, the date and time the message was sent, and its subject. The full header of an e-mail is hidden, so most people never see it. It can, however, be revealed and provide information on the route taken by the e-mail, including the originator's IP number. Here's how you can see a full header:

➤ In Microsoft Outlook, double-click on the e-mail. Then choose "Options," which is under "View" in the toolbar.

➤ In Outlook Express, click on the e-mail. Then click "Properties" under "File" in the toolbar. Select the "Details" tab.

➤ In Netscape, open the message. Then go to "Message Source" under "View" in the toolbar to display the header.

The first thing you will notice is the information revealed may not make much sense, but the tracking information you want is pretty easy to decipher. The key is in the sections beginning with the word "Received." You should see at least two of these postings. Further investigating will bring you right to the e-mail's originator—your cyberbully.

The following is an example:

Received: from
Mail.starrysky.com
(mailstarrysky.com
[123.312.54.12] by
mail.aol.com (8.8.5/8.7.2)
with ESMTP id EAA 12345 for [e
mail:johnsmith@aol.com];
Tue, 9 Sep 2006 13:10:30-0700
(MST)
Received: from joe.martin.com
(joe.martin.com
[124.213.45.11]) by
mail.starrysky.com (8.8.5) id
123A56; Tue, 9 Sep 2006 13:07:17
-0700 (MST)

Beth Ainsworth *(right)* helped push through an antibullying law in Indiana. Her daughter, Brittni *(left)*, was the victim of bullies at her high school.

The top part of the header tells the e-mail's recipient (John Smith). The name at the bottom is of the person who sent the e-mail. In this example, the sender is Joe Martin. Joe Martin's IP is 124.213.45.11.

Now you have the information to report Joe to his server. Most Internet Service Providers (ISPs) have a mailbox to receive e-mails that need to be investigated. Copy and paste the bully's message, along with all relevant information, to the ISP. Use the following addresses: abuse@ispname.com; postmaster@ispname.com; root@ispname.com; or admin@ispname.com. Just replace the ISP you discovered in the "ispname" part of the above e-mail addresses. Make sure you maintain the original e-mails for your records in case authorities want to see them.

If harassing material appears on a Web site, simply file a complaint through the "Contact Us" e-mail address on the site.

Next you'll want to keep all the abusive e-mails and messages. Print them out if you can. Create a folder on your desktop and label it "abuse." This way, you can save all the evidence without even opening it. Simply drag it to the folder, and store it there for safekeeping.

Cyberbullying is a violation of the "Terms of Use" of most Web sites, ISPs, and cell phone companies. You can file a complaint and provide the messages or a link to the material you've collected. Ask that the account be terminated and any harmful material removed. Most, if not all, ISPs have a mailbox set up to receive e-mails that need to be investigated.

Ending Cell Phone Harassment

If you are being harassed on your cell phone, the first step you should take is to report the harassment to your cell phone company. However, phone companies won't give information out freely. If you want to find out the identity of your cyberbully, you may have to contact the police. What you may want to consider doing before you file a police report is to change your phone number and see if that puts an end to the harassment.

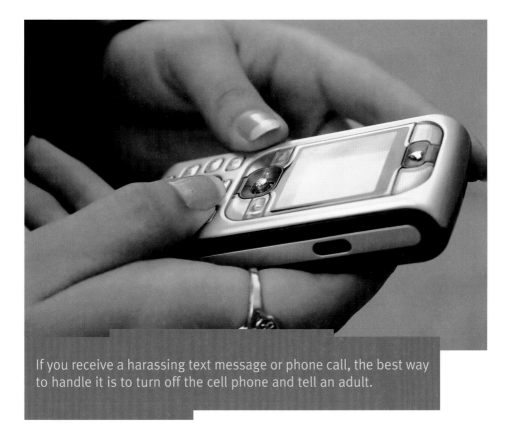

If you receive a harassing text message or phone call, the best way to handle it is to turn off the cell phone and tell an adult.

Taking Action

If you decide that you want to take legal action against a cyberbully, prepare carefully. If the cyberbully is someone you know, decide with a responsible adult what course of action to take. The options are many. You can report the abuse to online authorities, contact the bully's parents or guardians, contact school administrators and guidance counselors, and, if the

Ten Great Questions to Ask If You Think You're a Victim of Cyberbullying

1 How do I know if I am being cyberbullied?

2 What is the first thing I should do if I am receiving threatening messages?

3 How do I know when the cyberbullying is serious enough to call the police?

4 What are some effective ways to stop cyberbullying?

5 What should I say or do if the cyberbully confronts me?

6 Are there different ways of handling female cyberbullies versus male cyberbulllies?

7 Are there steps I can take to avoid being the target of cyberbullying in the first place?

8 What should I do if I suspect a friend is being cyberbullied?

9 What should I do if I witness cyberbullying as a bystander?

10 Is there any way to trace an anonymous cyberbully?

threats are serious enough, call the police. You may decide to do all of these things.

If the person who bullies you is a minor, and you and your parent or guardian decide to contact the cyberbully's parents, the best way is to mail a letter that includes copies of all the evidence. Make a firm, direct request in the letter that the harassment stop immediately and that all the harmful material be removed if it's posted online.

If the person's parents do not respond, you may want to contact an attorney. A lawyer can send a letter to the cyberbully's parents demanding that the harassment stop. He or she can also help file a lawsuit or help your parents file a small-claims action for financial damages and a requirement that the cyberbullying stop.

If the cyberbully or cyberbullies attend your school, make sure the school staff knows about the situation. All adults should be on the lookout for any bullying behavior or negative incidents so they can put a stop to them. Talk to your school counselor so that he or she can provide support by showing you how to deal with the bully in an assertive, not aggressive, way. Remember, it is important not to get emotional so that the bully doesn't feel any satisfaction.

Definitely contact the police if the cyberbullying appears to be a crime. Cyberbullying that involves threats, assault, coercion, obscene or harassing text messages, harassment or stalking, hate or bias crimes, creating or sending sexually explicit pictures, sexual exploitation, or taking a picture of someone in a private place are all crimes.

Don't React

It doesn't take much to turn an otherwise mild-mannered person into a cyberbully. All someone has to do is reply to an angry message he or she has received. Before either person knows it, a cyberwar has been declared. The objectives of bullies are power, control, and domination. They get a kick out of seeing you react. The cyberbully feels successful if he or she has provoked any reaction from you. After that, it's a matter of wearing you down. Keep in mind that bullying situations on the Web can quickly grow and involve more people. Instead of reacting to a flame mail or hate mail, look at it as a clue to the cyberbully's identity. Ask yourself, "What is this person revealing about himself or herself this time?" You may find important clues to identifying the culprit and stopping the behavior.

While it is difficult to ignore the cyberbully, try to do it for your own mental health. Block all future communications with him or her in e-mails and IM contact lists. Avoid going to Web sites where you have been attacked. Change your e-mail address, user name, or phone number. Be very careful with whom you share this information in the future. The best defense is to be alert at all times.

Chapter five

ARE THERE LAWS ON BULLYING AND CYBERBULLYING?

A recent survey of students estimated that one in ten has admitted to sending an abusive e-mail or text, according to cyberbullying.us. These students find new ways to harass their victims. Although cyberbullying is a relatively new problem, it is getting more attention from the media and the government. Legislators are working to pass laws that make electronic abuse a crime.

In 2005, the Anti-Bullying Act (H.R. 284) was introduced in the House of Representatives. The proposal requires states, districts, and schools to develop policies and programs to prevent and respond to bullying and harassment. It also allows schools to apply for federal grant money to create programs to educate students and school professionals about bullying. If the act becomes a law, it would

Tennessee senators Jim Bryson *(left)* and Diane Black helped pass a law requiring each of the state's school districts to adopt antibullying policies in 2005.

also permit schools to develop policies on use of personal computers and technology.

Currently, parents across the United States are gathering signatures on a petition to present to President George W. Bush, asking him to sign a federal antibullying law. There are presently twenty-six states that have antibullying laws in place and fifteen other states with similar laws in the works.

Free Speech Controversies

A person expresses his likes and dislikes on a Web site. If that information cruelly encourages harm against somebody else, is the person who wrote it a cyberbully? Does this form of free speech count as harassment? These are the same issues that lawmakers deal with when they consider rules governing online activities and harassment.

The First Amendment of the Constitution grants U.S. citizens the right to dissent. Protectors of free speech have argued that the main ideas of free speech tradition have been crucial in the process of building and maintaining a democratic government. Is there a limit to freedom of speech when it involves hurting others? When does a person's right to list his or her thoughts and feelings on a personal Web log actually become a form of cyberbullying?

There is a very fine line. According to the U.S. Supreme Court, one basis for regulating speech is proof that the speech in question may cause imminent, illegal action. This is called the "clear and present danger" test. For example, if a person swears in a chat room, aside from offending someone, no clear physical danger is present. However, if the person continued to use profanities and started to speak of others using those words along with direct threats, the situation now can be viewed as personalized and potentially dangerous. This would not pass the "clear and present danger" test.

The Center on Speech, Equality and Harm feels that the concept of free speech has been sorely abused. Officials there point to how laws regulate many categories of expression to prevent

Public awareness is the first step to curbing cyberbullying. Erika Harold of Illinois spent her 2003 reign as Miss America promoting antibullying programs.

harm or to encourage equality. These include instances such as when people plan crimes. They say the real issue is to determine whether the speech is harmful and, if it is, what can be done about it. The center rejects the idea of an Internet free of regulations. It is cyberspace, but cyberspace only exists with real people doing the communicating, it says.

Cyberbullying and Schools

Just because some laws are in place does not mean that they are effective. According to the Web site www.bullypolice.org, about 69 percent of students believe schools respond poorly to reports of bullying, both traditional and cyber. When schools intervene, they are often on very shaky legal ground. Many schools taking disciplinary action against a cyberbully have found themselves wrapped up in a lawsuit brought on by a civil liberties group or by an angry parent. These groups and parents believe that freedom of speech is a systematic right, no matter what an individual says or expresses. They believe that a person should have the right to post his or her opinions about somebody else, regardless of its effects. Many times, schools, when facing freedom of speech suits, lose.

Schools also have very limited authority to take action on events that take place off school grounds, outside of school hours, and that don't directly impact the school itself. Right now, they can only get involved in pursuing action against cyberbullies if there is a direct link between the bullying and the school. Otherwise, their hands are tied. For example, if a student is being bullied by a fellow classmate online or is being taunted through text messaging on a cell phone outside of school, the school can't punish the cyberbully. However, if the bully is caught doing the abuse on school grounds, using a school computer, or circulating digital pictures of a student at school, the staff can get involved.

Oftentimes, schools get involved without actually disciplining the cyberbully. Once reported by the victim, officials can call in both sets of parents and speak with them and the students to try to resolve the situation. They can't, however, discipline a cyberbullying student without his or her parents' consent if the abuse is happening outside of school.

Schools are also responding by limiting access to electronic devices in school, on school grounds, or at school-related functions. For example, after several students in the Boston, Massachusetts, public school system used school computers to send e-mail threats, pornography, and simulated hit lists to staff

Students in Pennsylvania participate in an antibullying lesson. More and more states are addressing the seriousness of bullying in schools through laws that seek to prevent and punish bullying.

and students, the superintendent banned the district's access to certain Web sites, including Hotmail and Yahoo! Mail. Other districts have followed suit by banning or limiting the use of IM, cell phones, and camera phones.

Individual Responsibility

Regardless of what laws get passed governing online behavior, change ultimately rests with you, the individual. How you act makes all the difference. It's easy to say mean things to others online. If someone gets you upset or does the mean thing first, you may think it's only fair to do it back. It isn't. Always remember that even though the Internet does not feel "real," and even though you may feel like you can be anyone you want online, there are still rules. If you break these rules, you could lose your e-mail, IM, or Internet account, or you could get into serious trouble with the law. Keep in mind that somebody with feelings is receiving and reading your messages. You have the power to prevent unnecessary distress for somebody else.

If you are a victim, don't be afraid to stand up for yourself. If you are a bystander, don't just watch—help the victim. Don't participate in any foul play against anyone else. It might be illegal, and it's definitely cruel.

bash board An online bulletin board on which individuals can post anything they want. Generally, posts are malicious and hateful statements directed against another person.

block To deny access. If a person is blocked from joining a chat, he or she usually receives a message that says access has been denied.

buddy list A collection of names or handles that represents friends or "buddies" within an instant-messaging or chat program. It informs a person of when his or her friends are online and available to chat.

bullying Any longstanding physical or psychological violence. One person or a group of people carry out the aggressive behavior repeatedly and over time.

chat An online conversation, typically between people who use nicknames instead of their real names. A person can read messages from others in the chat room and type in and send in his or her own messages in reply.

chat room A virtual room where groups of people send and receive messages on-screen. Popular chat rooms can have hundreds of people participating at the same time. A person's messages appear instantly as part of a real-time conversation. All of the people participating in a chat are listed by their nicknames or screen names somewhere on the screen.

cyberbullying Willfully or intentionally harming somebody through electronic text or a technological device.

cyberstalking Repeatedly "following" a victim around chat rooms, or repeatedly sending e-mails, text messages, or calling a victim so that the victim feels there is no escape.

cyberthreats Online material that raises concerns that the creator may intend to inflict harm or violence to himself or herself or someone else.

e-mail Electronic mail that allows Internet users to send and receive electronic text to and from other Internet users.

exclusion The barring of someone from an online group, like a buddy list.

flaming Sending angry, rude, or obscene messages directed at a person.

happy slapping An extreme form of bullying in which physical assaults are recorded on mobile phones and distributed to others.

harassment Unsolicited words or actions intended to annoy, alarm, or abuse another person.

impersonate To break into someone's e-mail account, pose as that person, and send messages to make the person look bad or get him or her into trouble.

instant messaging (IM) The act of communicating in real time between two or more people over a network such as the Internet.

Internet A worldwide network of computers communicating with each other via phone lines, satellite links, wireless networks, and cable systems.

ISP (Internet Service Provider) The company that provides an Internet connection to individuals or companies.

network Two or more computers that are connected so that they can communicate with each other.

outing Sharing somebody else's secrets or embarrassing information or images online.

social networking Web site Online service that brings people together by organizing them around a common interest and by providing them with an interactive environment of photos, Web logs, user profiles, and messaging systems. Examples include Facebook and MySpace.

spam Unsolicited electronic mail sent from someone the recipient does not know.

trolling Deliberately posting information to entice well-intentioned people to respond and contribute to a cruel discussion.

Web log An interactive Web journal or diary, the contents of which are posted online and viewable by some or all individuals. The act of updating a Web log is called blogging. A person who keeps a Web log is called a blogger.

American Foundation for Suicide Prevention
120 Wall Street, 22nd Floor
New York, NY 10005
(888) 333-AFSP (2377)
Web site: http://www.afsp.org
   This national nonprofit organization seeks to end
   occurrences of suicide through outreach and education.

Centre for Suicide Prevention
1202 Centre Street SE, Suite 320
Calgary, AB T2G 5A5
Web site: http://www.suicideinfo.ca
   This Canadian organization offers information about suicide
   and trains people for suicide outreach work.

Parry Aftab
1 Bridge Street
Irvington-on-Hudson, NY 10533
(201) 463-8663
E-mail: parry@aftab.com
Web site: http://www.aftab.com/cyberbullying.htm
   Parry Aftab, a private Internet lawyer, runs a site that
   deals with cyberbullying.

Samaritans Suicide Prevention Center
P.O. Box 5228

Albany, NY 12205

(518) 689-HOPE (4673)

Web site: http://www.timesunion.com/communities/samaritans
This nonprofit group offers support and education to those
contemplating suicide.

Hotlines

Cybertipline: (800) 843-5678

National Suicide Hotline: (800) SUICIDE (784-2433)

Youthline: (800) 246-4646

In Canada

Kid's Help Phone: (800) 668-6868

Web Sites

Due to the changing nature of Internet links, Rosen Publishing
has developed an online list of Web sites related to the subject
of this book. This site is updated regularly. Please use this link
to access the list:

http://www.rosenlinks.com/faq/cybu

For Further Reading

Aftab, Parry. *The Parents Guide to Protecting Your Children in Cyberspace.* New York, NY: McGraw-Hill, 2000.

Coloroso, Barbara. *The Bully, the Bullied, and the Bystander: From Preschool to High School—How Parents and Teachers Can Help Break the Cycle of Violence.* New York, NY: HarperCollins, 2003.

Dellasega, Cheryl, and Charisse Nixon, Ph.D. *Girl Wars: 12 Strategies That Will End Female Bullying.* New York, NY: Fireside, 2003.

Garbarino, James, and Ellen deLara, Ph.D. *And Words Can Hurt Forever: How to Protect Adolescents from Bullying, Harassment, and Emotional Violence.* New York, NY: The Free Press, 2002.

Willard, Nancy E. *Cyberbullying and Cyberthreats: Responding to the Challenge of Online Social Cruelty, Threats, and Distress.* Eugene, OR: Center for Safe and Responsible Internet, 2006.

Aftab, Parry. "Wired Kids, Inc." Retrieved April 12, 2006 (http://www.aftab.com/cyberbullyingpage.htm).

Berson, I. R., M. J. Berson, and J. M. Ferron. "Emerging Risks of Violence in the Digital Age: Lessons for Educators from an Online Study of Adolescent Girls in the United States." *Journal of School Violence*, Vol. 1, No. 2, 2002, pp. 51–71.

Brown, Eric. "Cyberbullying: Today's Bullies Hide Behind Technology." *Leader-Post*, January 7, 2006.

Carlisle, Randall. "BYU Animators and Utah's First Lady Help Take a Bite Out of Internet Crime." ABC Channel 4. April 10, 2006.

Center for Safe and Responsible Internet Use. "Cyberbullying or Cyberthreat Situation Review Process." Retrieved April 12, 2006 (http://cyberbully.org and http://csriu.org).

Dyrli, Odvard Egil. "Cyberbullying: Online Bullying Affects Every School District (The Online Edge)." *District Administration*, Vol. 41, No. 9, September 2005, p. 63.

Field, Michael, and Tim Field. "Cyberbullying on the Internet: Cyber Bullies, Cyber Bullying, Flame Mail, Hate Mail." Retrieved April 12, 2006 (http://www.bullyonline.org).

Fratt, Lisa. "Making Cyberspace Safer." *District Administration*, Vol. 42, No. 3, March 2006, p. 34.

Government of Alberta. "Bully Free Alberta." Retrieved April 12, 2006 (www.bullyfreealberta.ca/bullying.htm).

Hinduja, Sameer, and Justine W. Patchin, Ph.D. "Cyberbullying: A Preliminary Profile of Offending and Victimization." November 2005. Retrieved May 2006 (http://www. cyberbullying.us).

Keith, Susan, and Michelle E. Martin. "Cyberbullying: Creating a Culture of Respect in a Cyber World." *Reclaiming Children and Youth*, Vol. 13, No. 4, Winter 2005, pp. 224–225.

McGee, Marianne Kolbasuk. "Cyberbullying Eyed as Latest E-Threat by Washington." *InternetWeek*, May 25, 2005.

National Crime Prevention Council. "Stop Cyberbullying." Retrieved April 12, 2006 (http://www.mcgruff.org/Grownups/ StopCyberbullying.htm).

National Institute of Child Health & Human Development. "Bullying Statistics." Retrieved April 12, 2006 (http://www. atriumsoc.org/pages/bullyingstatistics.html).

Page, Chris. "Striking Back at the Cyberbullies." *BBC Five Live Radio Report*, April 16, 2006.

Powderly, Henry. "Child Abuse Prevention Services to Promote Internet Safety." *Long Island Business News*, January 28, 2005.

Sparling, Polly. "Mean Machines: New Technologies Let the Neighborhood Bully Taunt You Anywhere, Anytime." *Current Health 2*, Vol. 31, No. 1, September 1, 2004, p. 11.

Splete, H. "Technology Can Extend the Reach of a Bully." *Family Practice News*, Vol. 35, No.12, June 15, 2005, p. 31.

Toppo, Greg. "Girls Using Text Messaging to Bully." *USA Today*, April 17, 2006.

Willard, Nancy. "Flame Retardant." *School Library Journal*, April 2006.

Index

About the Author

Teri Breguet is a writer who resides in Russell, Massachusetts, with her husband and two children. A newspaper and broadcast journalist, she also lobbies for children's safety at the Boston statehouse.

Photo Credits

Cover © www.istockphoto.com/Galina Barskaya; p. 5 © Jennifer Brown/ Star Ledger/Corbis; p. 9 Sherri Smith/Shutterstock.com; p. 11 © age fotostock/Superstock; p. 16 Shutterstock.com; p. 19 © Virgo/zefa/ Corbis; p. 21 © Jennie Woodcock, Reflections Photolibrary/Corbis; p. 26 © www.istockphoto.com/ericsphotography; p. 29 © Bob Child/AP/Wide World Photos; p. 33 Tan Kian Khoon/Shutterstock.com; p. 37 Galina Barskaya/Shutterstock.com; p. 41 © Tom Strattman/AP/Wide World Photos; p. 43 © www.istockphoto.com/Oleg Prikhodko; p. 48 © John Russell/AP/Wide World Photos; p. 50 © Toyokazu Kosugi/AP/Wide World Photos; p. 52 © Jacqueline Larma/AP/Wide World Photos.

Editor: Jun Lim; Designer: Evelyn Horovicz
Photo Researcher: Hillary Arnold